TURTLE IN PARADISE

The Graphic
Novel

ALSO BY JENNIFER L. HOLM

BY JENNIFER L. HOLM AND MATTHEW HOLM

ALSO BY SAVANNA GANUCHEAU

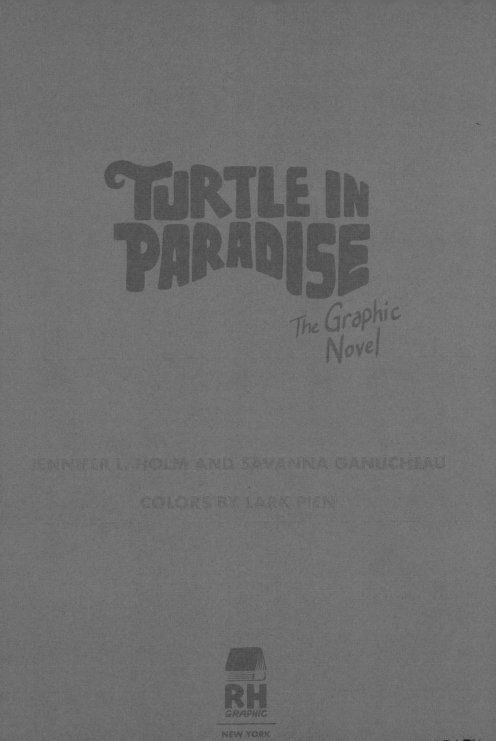

TURTLE IN PARADISE

The Graphic Novel

JENNIFER L. HOLM AND SAVANNA GANUCHEAU

COLORS BY LARK PIEN

RH GRAPHIC

NEW YORK

Photo credits: p. 235: © Bettmann/CORBIS. p. 236: Library of Congress, Prints and Photographs Division, FSA/OWI Collection, LC-USF34-026281-PDLC. p. 237 (top): Monroe County Library. p. 237 (bottom): Personal collection of Cathy Porter, used by permission. p. 238: State Archives of Florida.

Text copyright © 2021 by Jennifer L. Holm
Jacket and interior illustrations copyright © 2021 by Savanna Ganucheau

All rights reserved. Published in the United States by RH Graphic, an imprint of Random House Children's Books, a division of Penguin Random House LLC, New York.

RH Graphic with the book design is a trademark of Penguin Random House LLC.

Visit us on the web and sign up for our newsletter! RHKidsGraphic.com • @RHKidsGraphic

Educators and librarians, for a variety of teaching tools, visit us at RHTeachersLibrarians.com

Library of Congress Cataloging-in-Publication Data is available upon request.
ISBN 978-0-593-12630-1 (pbk) — ISBN 978-0-593-12631-8 (trade) —
ISBN 978-0-593-12632-5 (library binding) — ISBN 978-0-593-12633-2 (ebook)

Designed by Patrick Crotty

MANUFACTURED IN CHINA
10 9 8 7 6 5 4 3 2 1
First Edition

A comic on every bookshelf.

Turtle in Paradise was drawn and colored digitally in Photoshop. It was lettered using the font Smiling Cat.

For my Conch cuzzies, Kurt and Monica —J.H.

Conch

Pronunciation: 'känk, 'känch
Function: noun
1: any of various large spiral-shelled marine
gastropod mollusks (as of the genus *Strombus*)
2: often capitalized: a native or resident of the Florida Keys

—*Merriam-Webster's Collegiate Dictionary,*
11th edition

Rotten Kids

Everyone thinks children are sweet as Necco Wafers.

But I've lived long enough to know the truth.

Paradise Lost

Lucky as an Orphan

I used to feel sorry for orphans...

...but Little Orphan Annie got adopted by Daddy Warbucks...

CREAK

That's just about as lucky as it gets.

I bet she doesn't have to worry about being sent to a house that's tiny and dark and smells like sour milk.

The Conch
Telegraph

Can You Spare
a Nickel, Pal?

Truth of the
Matter

Duval Street is like a prettified version of Key West. Kermit tells me that they're trying to get tourists to come down here, which is why it's all fixed up.

There's even a movie theater.
Too bad it's showing a
Shirley Temple picture.

The Lost Love

A Big, Happy Family

The Diaper Gang
Knows

The Man of
the House

Dear Turtle,

How are you, baby? I miss you something awful.

Mrs. Budnick never sleeps and doesn't care if anybody else does, either. She thinks nothing of waking me up in the middle of the night to make her tea or toast. I'm so tired I can barely see straight. The only thing that keeps me going is thinking of you.

Someday this will all be behind us, I promise. I've been thinking that maybe I can become an actress. Can't you just see my name in lights?

All I need to do now is get a screen test with Warner Brothers.

Love Always,
Mama

Oh, Smokey... Mama's head is so high in the clouds, I'm surprised she doesn't bump into Amelia Earhart.

Who's that coming down the lane?

What?

Thought you knew everyone by now, Tortoise.

Whenever Archie comes back from a sales trip, it's just like Christmas. He buys treats for me and Mama.

Uncle Vernon doesn't buy treats like Archie, but things are different with him in the house.

He doesn't say much at all.

But I like him.

Ladies Who Lunch

Hard Times

HAAAAAAAAAAA!!

Sounded like Ma. Do you think someone's tick-tocking us?

WAAAAAA

GET IT OFF ME!

GET IT OFF ME!

Believing in
Monsters

Peek

In my opinion, the fellas who make Hollywood pictures are really just salesmen. Instead of peddling girdles, they sell chills and thrills.

WIPE

Even comic strips want you to believe an orphan would be adopted by a millionaire.

And perhaps I could believe that.

This being where Blacke Caesar Putte his Treassure

But to believe in this...

SNAP

That'd be like believing in bloodsucking vampires and mad scientists bringing dead men to life.

Lying, Stealing, No-Good Kids

A Dream
Come True

The Rescue Party

A Hollywood
Ending

Snore

I seem to be missing a boat.

. . . .

We been looking for you kids since Minerva raised the alarm. But we had to put in once the hurricane started blowing.

That was a hurricane?!

Sure was, Miss Turtle.

Paradise Found

No more scrubbing floors for me! You should have seen Mrs. Budnick's face when I quit, baby!

Now me, you, and Archie are gonna get us a lovely plot of land in Georgia. A perfect place for the Bellewood.

Mama, can I ask you something?

Of course, baby.

How well did you know Slow Poke?

• • •

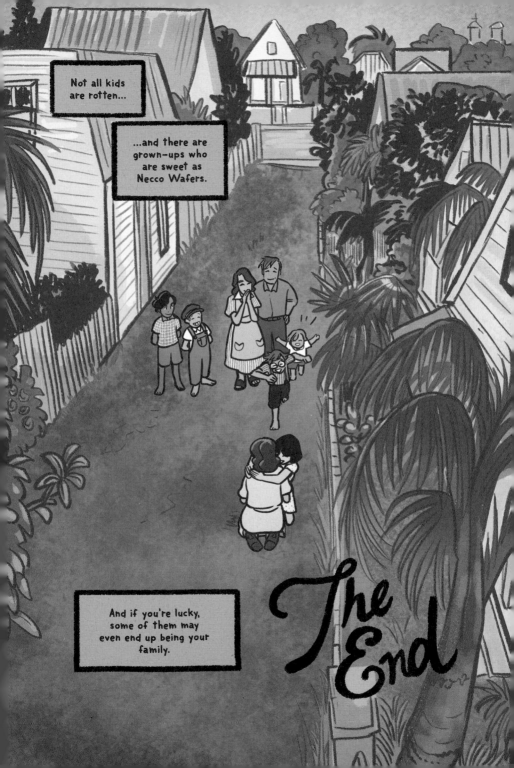

Acknowledgments

Warm thanks for everyone who helped Turtle find her way home,
especially the Key West Art and Historical Society, Kurt and Monica
Lewin, Michelle Nagler, Gina Gagliano, and Lark Pien.

—J.H.

Thank you to the supportive team at Random House Graphic, Lark
Pien, my friends, and my wonderful partner, Stephen.

—S.G.

About the Authors

Jennifer L. Holm's great-grandmother emigrated from the Bahamas to Key West in 1897. She has written two Key West novels: *Turtle in Paradise* and *Full of Beans*, which won the Scott O'Dell Award for Historical Fiction. She is a *New York Times* bestselling author and the recipient of three Newbery Honors for her novels *Turtle in Paradise*, *Our Only May Amelia*, and *Penny from Heaven*. She is also the author of other highly praised books, including *The Fourteenth Goldfish* and *The Third Mushroom*. With her brother Matthew Holm, she is the co-creator of the Eisner Award–winning Babymouse series, the Squish series, and the Sunny Side Up graphic novels.

Savanna Ganucheau is a comic artist from New Orleans. She co-authored her first graphic novel, *Bloom*, in 2019 with Kevin Panetta. *Bloom* received a distinction from the Junior Library Guild and a GLAAD award nomination, and was Amazon's pick for Best Graphic Novel of the Year. Savanna has been creating comics since she was in third grade, and she self-published her work in local comic book shops throughout high school. Savanna has also contributed to such comic series as Adventure Time, Lumberjanes, Jem and the Holograms, and The Backstagers.

Lark Pien is the colorist of *American Born Chinese*, *Boxers and Saints*, *Dragon Hoops*, *Stargazing*, *Sunny Side Up*, *Swing It, Sunny*, and *Sunny Rolls the Dice*. She has authored three picture books and is the creator of the Long Tail Kitty series and *Mr. Elephanter*. Lark began making mini-comics in 1997 and is making them still today. You can find occasional tweets and IG posts at @larkpien.

a Note from Jennifer L. Holm

Turtle in Paradise was inspired by my Conch great-grandmother, Jennie Lewin Peck, who emigrated with her family from the Bahamas to Key West in the late 1800s. As a child, I heard about Spanish limes and sugar apple ice cream and the importance of shaking out your shoes to avoid scorpions. My family is related to the Curry family of Key West, after whom Curry Lane is named.

Many families suffered hardship during the Great Depression, and it was not unusual for parents to leave home in search of work or for children to be cared for by relatives. Then, as now, entertainment was a great distraction, and movies, radio shows, and the funny pages provided much amusement for everyone. Little Orphan Annie, Shirley Temple, and the Shadow were all superstars in their day.

Shirley Temple popping through a 1935 calendar

At the height of the Depression, Key West was in economic ruin, with the majority of the population on public relief. The town officially declared bankruptcy. FERA, the Federal Emergency Relief Administration, came into Key West in 1934 with the intent of reinvigorating the economy by marketing it as a tourist attraction. Key West was on its way to recovery when what became known as the Labor Day Hurricane struck on September 2, 1935. While the Lower Keys and Key West were largely spared, the Middle and Upper Keys bore the brunt of the storm, with terrible loss of life.

Searching for pirate loot has always been a popular pastime in the Keys. Jeane Porter, in her book *Key West: Conch Smiles*, writes, "When I was a little girl in the early '30s everybody in Key West had a treasure story." While actually finding pirate treasure may seem far-fetched, historical rumors abound. In Charlotte Niedhauk's account of living in the Florida Keys during this time, *Charlotte's Story*, she relates the tale circulating around Key West of a sponge fisherman who mysteriously disappeared with his family to South America after finding the treasure of a pirate named Black Caesar. Whether Black Caesar ever visited the Keys is still a matter of speculation.

Pepe's Café is a beloved institution in Key West. It still exists, although it is no longer on Duval Street.

Pepe's Café, Key West, Florida, circa 1938

Key West children posing on the docks with five turtles and a pile of sponges in the background

The sponging industry and turtle kraals are remnants of the past, but they were once thriving industries. Nicknaming was a Key West tradition, and the nicknames came in all styles. The scorpion sting suffered by Aunt Minnie was inspired by an actual incident.

Likewise, some of the characters had their inspiration in actual people. The writer Ernest Hemingway was one of Key West's most famous residents. He was in Key West when the Labor Day Hurricane struck, and he witnessed the aftermath firsthand and wrote about it. In true Key West fashion, he had a nickname among the locals—Papa. Kermit was inspired by my cousin Kermit Lewin. The real Kermit suffered rheumatic fever as a child and grew up to become the mayor of Key West in the 1960s. He famously tricked Jimmy the ice cream man with the "nickel in the bottom of the cup" trick to get free ice cream, and he did tick-tock people. Killie the Horse and Jimmy were actual local characters of Key West.

The real Kermit (left) circa 1930, with the family friend who inspired Pork Chop

Finally, the Diaper Gang's secret diaper-rash formula is a family remedy I have used on my own babies' bungys. (It also works on mosquito bites.)

My family's recollections, and those of many other Conchs, provided the details of everyday life in this book, and I am grateful to them all for sharing their memories.

Jenni

A typical Conch neighborhood in Key West, circa 1935

A Note from Savanna Ganucheau

Historical fiction was my favorite genre throughout middle school, and I know that a Turtle-aged Savanna would have loved to read *Turtle in Paradise*.

When starting this project, the biggest challenge was truly appreciating a place that I have never been to, and imagining what it was like well before I was born. Much of my time was spent looking up specific details with little photographic evidence, like the exact species of sponge they used to harvest in Key West. It is hard to express the excitement I felt when I finally found a map of 1930s Key West and began to piece together Turtle's exact steps through the town. This book was a crash course in visually researching a historical location.

Many of the visuals and experiences in Key West really spoke to me. When I was Turtle's age, I lived in a small beach town in Mississippi, and I dreamed of an adventure just like hers. The neighbors called me the marine biologist because I was always on the beach, investigating creatures that would wash up on shore at the end of their life in the gulf. Turtle is similarly curious, and I know I would have connected with her when I was younger.

The development of *Turtle in Paradise* was quick and intense, and I've read so much about Key West that it truly feels like I've been there. From the history of the Bahama Village to struggling through historical boat research, I've learned about Key West through many lenses. I can only hope I did the Conchs' unique town justice.

To the readers, I hope that you enjoyed this book and that your mind, like Turtle's, stays curious and questioning.

Making the Art of Turtle in Paradise with Savanna Ganucheau

Here's how a page of *Turtle in Paradise* came together from start to finish! Everyone's process is different, but this is how I work on comic pages.

Step 1: Thumbnails

After the script is finished, I work on thumbnails. This is when I figure out where the panels and characters will go on the page. This step is very helpful to see if the page works well with the surrounding pages.

Step 2: Pencils

The next step is to finalize the layout and sketch the figures and backgrounds. In this example, you can see how I changed things to show more of the house and added a reaction shot of Turtle entering.

Step 3: Inks

The inks step is where everything gets polished. During this step, the lettering is also finalized.

Step 4: Colors

After I finish inks and everything is approved by the editor, I hand the page over to the colorist, Lark!

From Lark
Turtle and company were colored in Photoshop, with a few Kyle T. Webster brushes. I like to color scene by scene, rather than page by page!

Concept Art

My first-ever drawing of Turtle and Smokey, accompanied by the foliage of a Key West lane.

Here are the initial concepts for the Diaper Gang and the grown-ups. Turtle has a bit more personality here than above. For the grown-ups, it was interesting to focus on a family resemblance between Sadie and Minnie, while incorporating some of their features in Turtle's face as well.

Turtle in Paradise
THE DIAPER GA

Turtle   Beans   Pork chop   kermit   Ira   Buddy

Nana Philly

with hat

Nana Philly was the last character
I designed. It was important to me that
she resembles the rest of the Giffords,
while also conveying a stern appearance.

Sadiebelle Minnie Slow Poke Archie Vernon

Early Cover Concepts

Adapted by Savanna Ganucheau
Original story by Jenni Holm

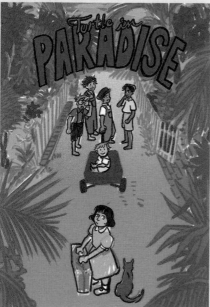

An adaptation of the *New York Times*
bestselling, Newbery Honor-winning novel

Turtle in Paradise

JENNI HOLM
SAVANNA GANUCHEAU

FIND YOUR VOICE
WITH ONE OF THESE EXCITING GRAPHIC NOVELS

1447